SPINE-CHILLERS

NORTH WEST TERRORS

Edited By Lisa Adlam

Years of YoungWriters

First published in Great Britain in 2017 by:

Coltsfoot Drive
Peterborough
PE2 9BF
Telephone: 01733 890066
Website: www.youngwriters.co.uk

FOREWORD

Welcome to 'Spine-Chillers –North West Terrors'.
For our latest Young Writers' competition, open to 11-18 year-olds, we set students the challenge of writing a spooky story using 100 words or fewer. Ghost stories really grip the imagination and it was clear that our writers enjoyed trying to terrify their readers!
Inside, you will find plenty of tales to give you goosebumps with sinister shadows, spooky graveyards and ghostly presences. Students have shown great skill in their use of mood and setting. Most stories are intended to be scary but there are some that turn the tale on its head, with an unexpected comedic ending!
The response to this competition was fantastic and it has been great to see what the pupils have come up with. Well done to everyone whose work has been published and I hope it encourages you to keep writing creatively in the future.

Lisa Adlam

CONTENTS

Chelsea Starkey (13) 66
Angel Minto (12) 67
Joshua James Jones (13) 68
Chloe Bastin (12) 69

ULLSWATER COMMUNITY COLLEGE, PENRITH

Joel Ogden (14) 70
Ben Perris (12) 71
Savannah Edwards-Lynch (13) 72
Nathan Jack Lee (12) 73
Eleanor Jane Farthing (12) 74
Ben Sharpe (13) 75
James Jones (12) 76
Ben Thompson (14) 77
Fern Denney (13) 78
Kacper Zbikowski (13) 79
Lauren Adams (13) 80
Chloe Earl (14) 81
Kate Hornby (12) 82
Ben Devlin (14) 83
Charlie Kirkland (13) 84
Ellie Lloyds (11) 85
Hugh Burne (14) 86
Joseph Thomas Gate (13) 87
Arthur Bowman (12) 88
Taylor Teasdale (12) 89
Naomi Purdham (14) 90
Romney Thompson (12) 91
Holly Gate (12) 92
Edward Greed (12) 93
Lilly Nulty (11) 94
Eve Edmondson (14) 95
Sarah Hale (13) 96
Louie Bellas (15) 97
Anna Dinsdale (14) 98
Nicole Bailey (11) 99
Ryan Mole (14) 100
Emma Noble (13) 101
Carys Benn (13) 102
Fraser Little (12) 103
Alice Bayliffe (15) 104
Daniel Monkhouse (14) 105
Lennox Rylands (15) 106
Dylan Lourie (14) 107

Rowan McCarthy (15) 108
Craig Bottomley (14) 109
Freya Weston (14) 110
Ryan Eveleigh (12) 111
Roxanne Hodgson (14) 112
Matthew Wills (15) 113
Lauren Caris (12) 114
Isabelle Boothman (12) 115
Holly Wilmot (15) 116
Gabrielle Jane Bailey (13) 117
Molly Coward (14) 118
Kelly Noble (14) 119
Arran Barber (14) 120
Tyson Weir (14) 121
Elizabeth Jackson (11) 122
Charlie Felton (12) 123
Isabelle Leonard (12) 124
Niamh Brenan (12) 125
Samantha Westgarth (12) 126
Ruby Eden (12) 127
Rosie Horne (14) 128
Teri Ann Chadwick-Whalley (13) 129
Nathan Savage (15) 130
Charlie Grace Healey (13) 131
Adam Walton (15) 132
Sinead Thompson (12) 133
Dan Harrison (15) 134
Travis Thomas Hutchcroft (12) 135
Elenna Bullock (12) 136
Kieron Lee Phillips-Craig (14) 137
Hannah Emmerson (12) 138
Darcy C C Lee (12) 139
Charlotte Holliday (14) 140
Megan Fawcett (14) 141
Elliot Kitchen (13) 142
Daisy Blundell (12) 143
Summer Latham (14) 144
Kitty Nicolson (13) 145
Lola Elizabeth Hewitt (11) 146
Jack Graham (12) 147
Louis Davidson (12) 148
Kieran Jamie Dixon (12) 149
Kyle Strand (14) 150
Lily Kitching (12) 151
Aaron Cavaghan (12) 152
Lucy Hodgson (14) 153

THE MINI SAGAS

Sounds

The blaze of the crescent moon crawled upon me. It was as dark as space but with no stars. I, a humble man, had my children waiting for me but I knew I wasn't coming back. How I got there, I don't know. All I remember is that I missed my wife, I missed my children, Frankie and Jack. They were too young to be alone. All around me I saw dead trees. The devil sucked the life from them. I felt the wind warning me. I still remember my children. I suddenly heard sirens and screams from the Devil...

Henry Mitchell Maw (12)
Birkdale High School, Southport

Friend Or Foe?

We wandered aimlessly and loudly down the road, protected by the anonymity of the dark. Bill began to stomp noisily next to me, then stopped. 'Wow!' I exclaimed. Before us was a hole in the road.

'How deep do you think it is?' Bill murmured, pushing aside a road block.

'I dunno.'

We stared at the unfathomable black depths. There was a low chuckle. Menacing. I whipped around.

'Let's get out of here!' I whispered, but Bill wouldn't move. He gazed, transfixed, deep into the pit. 'Bill!' He turned with an unnatural grin. Then I realised the chuckle was his...

Elliot James Brown (13)

Birkdale High School, Southport

THE REFLECTION

Andrew was surprised that he was given something in his aunt's will. He looked at the mirror that he had been given, he put it into his room and slept. He awoke and felt a cool breeze. He saw the mirror, a face was reflected on it - it was his grandad's!

The following day, Andrew found out that his grandad had passed away. He asked one of the locals about the mirror, apparently the person who appeared in it would die the next day.

That night, the face in the mirror, to his surprise and horror, was his own...

NATHAN SCALES (14)

Birkdale High School, Southport

Forgotten Surgeon

Fallen branches crunched, there was whistling from the howling wind. I hobbled towards the closest shelter. The deserted hospital door creaked open after an apprehensive push. Edging further down the corridor, I began regretting my choice. I turned towards the exit - no escape. There was a scuttle along the floor, then a slam from the door; something had followed me in. Darkness flooded the building. My heart began to pound. An ear-piercing shriek punctured the silence of the corridors. An object flew into my skull. I awoke to see him gazing over me.
'Time for surgery, Master Roberts.'

Samuel Roberts (14)
Birkdale High School, Southport

Come Play With Us

My footsteps creaked on the broken floorboards of the forgotten orphanage. I trod carefully to avoid the shattered glass that carpeted the floor. This place had been abandoned for years, so why were my footsteps not the only ones there? I continued down the dark, dilapidated hall but froze when I heard the eerie sound of a child's laugh. I wasn't alone. I inched down the corridor, towards the candlelit room. I was a few steps away from where the sound had emanated from. My heartbeat intensified as I stepped into the doorway of the room.
'Come play with us.'

Ethan Mosson (14)
Birkdale High School, Southport

THE SNOW CABIN

I was home alone. The sound of snow hitting the window was relaxing until I felt a strange feeling. Suddenly, something other than snow hit my window, then I heard the door opening. I thought it was my friend Tommo, but when I called his name, there was no answer. I looked out of my room. I slammed my door shut and hid under the bed, I looked to my left and saw an eye looking back. I screamed a horrific scream. Two hands clasped my mouth shut as I was dragged from under the bed.
'Don't say a word.'

TAYLOR STANBROOK (13)
Birkdale High School, Southport

THE MUSIC BOX

I awoke in a cold room. Cockroaches ran along the walls. Suddenly, the door flew open, revealing a narrow hallway. The door on the right was blocked off. The only other door was at the end of the left side. I heard the chime of a music box. For some reason, I was drawn to it. As I got closer, my watch suddenly froze. I felt a chill on my neck, like someone was behind me, breathing on me. I was too scared to turn around.

Finally, I reached the door and as I turned the handle, the music stopped...

LEWIS HILL (14)
Birkdale High School, Southport

The Notes

There were no birds fluttering through the willow of the trees. Sensing something was wrong, I immediately sat up, noticing a torn note: 'Once you see it, there's no escape'. An abrupt shiver ran through my spine. Tentative, I got up and started wandering around my apartment. All of a sudden, another note appeared: 'Let me in!' Running for the door, there lay another note: 'The more you deny, the stronger I get!' Frozen in place, I fell into darkness. Waking up in a white room, I faintly made out the words: 'It's a miracle, he's survived cancer'...

Vlad Ungureanu (14)

Birkdale High School, Southport

THE DEEP

The submarine slowly submerged into the dark depths of the Atlantic Ocean. The captain appeared on deck to see something circling around the submarine. He sent six divers out to investigate. Suddenly, two divers' heart rates disappeared and a gruesome scream could be heard through the radio. The captain bellowed down the radio, 'Get out of there, now!' Scared and alone, one of the divers had lost his way and came across the corpse of his former colleague. The bones were ripped and blood was spilt everywhere. He heard a mighty roar and soon all that was left was blood.

KAMAL AMIR KHAN (12)
Birkdale High School, Southport

THE LONE HOUSE

Walking through the murky, dank forest, he came across the derelict house. His curiosity overwhelmed him and he reached towards the huge, rotting oak doors. He cautiously stepped into the eerie, chilly room, the only source of light coming from next door. He started walking forwards... *bang!* The door behind him slammed. He continued towards the light slowly, barely making a noise. He reached the dim room. It was empty apart from a lone box. Still curious, the boy inched towards the box and reached for it with a shaking hand. He gripped the box and opened it...

JOSHUA HARDING (13)

Birkdale High School, Southport

A Nightmare From Darkness And Beyond

The light set and darkness came. There were creaks from floorboards and screams from rooms. A light flashed. Nothing was to be seen. The old Victorian house seemed to be alive. Lost and helpless, I set about wandering through the wooden maze. As I entered the master bedroom, I heard a bang. Shaking, I was nervous and anxious. I didn't dare turn around to see what lay in the horrors of the room. With suspense in the atmosphere, an old music box started playing. I looked around with great fear. Everything died down. A figure crept out of the darkness...

Jamie Roberts (13)
Birkdale High School, Southport

An Empty Corridor

I peered through the cracked window before I braved the eerie corridor. The door creaked as it was opened, but the noise was not from the door I had opened, for it was already shut. It came from the other end of the corridor. The end was sheltered in darkness. The place was empty. It couldn't be anyone, surely. Could it? The lights near me started to flicker. Footsteps approached. I heard the chilling breathing of another human. He entered the flickering light. It went off. On, off, on, off. He got closer every time. He stood directly before me...

Ethan Mobbs-Pursell (14)

Birkdale High School, Southport

DON'T LET HIM GET YOU

The country lane was desolate. The mental asylum lurked between the overhanging trees. As I climbed through the eerie hole in the window, my pulse increased with every minute. Alone, I was vulnerable and weak. As I crept past the nursery, I heard a sound that stopped my heart beating. An innocent child's voice spoke from inside the room. As I reluctantly brushed my hand across the handle, I dragged my body inside. A child covered in white silk was facing the chalkboard. She picked up the chalk and slowly wrote, 'Don't let him get you'.

GEORGE ROBERT SAUNDRY (14)
Birkdale High School, Southport

WHAT LURKS IN THE SHADOWS

I crept through the encompassing darkness into a desolate ward. Dilapidated hospital beds lined the walls. Suddenly, a blood-curdling scream pierced the silence, eerily echoing through the hollow building. I heard the sudden creaking of wheels as a rickety bed emerged from the shadows. Then I saw it, a shadowy, looming shape trailing behind the bed. Moonlight danced around it. I lunged for the door, it refused to open. As I slammed my fists on the door, shrieking for my life, I felt an icy-cold breath on my back as something clasped around my neck...

NATHAN CREWE (14)

Birkdale High School, Southport

GHOST SHIP

The ship groaned and lunged onto its side. I tripped up, fell and stumbled into the storage room. A strange gushing noise filled the air, and I felt a strange tingling sensation in my feet. Freezing Atlantic water rapidly filled the room. I shuffled through the darkness, making my way to the door. I tugged at the handle, but it was locked. 'Help!' I screamed. I waited, no reply. In the darkness of the room there was a skeleton laid in the corner. It had an old wooden sign draped around its neck. Red liquid declared: 'You're next'.

LEWIS ROSE (13)
Birkdale High School, Southport

And...

I crept into a seemingly empty house. Upon the walls lay long-forgotten family photos. Sunlight streaked through the jagged windows and a slight wheezing began. A door creaked open and I peered inside. A rotten staircase led down to an eerie room. I was drawn downstairs for an unknown reason. The steps crumbled and sent me tumbling down. As I reached the bottom, my back struck against something cold. I turned my head and saw a flickering movement. As I attempted to push myself up, my leg faltered. A rotten hand grabbed me, flecked with blood...

Benjamin Harvey (14)
Birkdale High School, Southport

THE MINE

Night darkened the mine, it was a pitch-black abyss. I, along with the others, walked down to the large elevator shaft that would take us to the surface. As I walked onto it, I felt the searing metal chamber boil my insides. But as the elevator reached the 500 mark, the cable (weakened after twenty years) finally snapped, sending us into hell once again. As we fell, I heard the electric cables rip apart, sending volts shooting across the metal. Finally, it crashed down, sending the elevator, myself and my colleagues into the depths of Hell.

SAM BELLAMY (13)
Birkdale High School, Southport

THE ROOM

I wake up and find myself in an unfamiliar room, in an unfamiliar bed. Unsettled, I hear an eerie knocking at the door. It is open. I tentatively seek its source. I see eyes in the darkness, gone within a second. There's a rush of wind, something brushes my leg. There's the patter of feet in the distance. I follow the ominous sound of singing through the desolate hall. As I approach, the sound gets deeper. From a dark child's room, I hear it. It's a rocking horse with a bloodied handprint. It still rocks in the empty room...

ELLIOT RATCLIFFE (14)
Birkdale High School, Southport

It's Behind You

The rusted metal gates opened with no human force. I walked down the winding path to the door of the dilapidated house. The cracked wooden door towered above me and I pushed it open. The creak echoed through every room. My 'Hello?' disappeared into the darkness of the corridor. Mist seeped through the cracked window. I heard walking getting closer and closer. Looking outside the window, I saw the noose swaying in the wind, on the branch of the tree. It waited for someone. I looked back to see my worst nightmare looking at me...

Tobias Lea
Birkdale High School, Southport

No Hiding Now

A child is lying in his bedroom, peering over his sheets, watching the wardrobe at the end of his bed. The door is ajar. Narrow, frosty lips shush him. He hides in the sheets, seeing feet crawl over his bed. They go. Claws scrape across the floorboards. The child comes out from the sheets, looking around, terrified. There's scratching and tapping everywhere. His eyes focus on the room's darkest corner as flakes of skin drift to the ground. It drops to the ground. Its cracked skin clutches onto him, there's no hiding now...

Solomon Palmer (14)

Birkdale High School, Southport

ALONE?

Lost, alone, it was my only option. I approached the boarded window of the abandoned house. At least I thought it was. I breached the window. Silence. I struck a match but it wasn't long until it was out. I went to light another but it was halted by the sound of chains being dragged along the floor above me. The ceiling started to creak with the weight of footsteps. I turned to see the window was boarded back up. The footsteps were silenced. I felt a breeze upon my neck. There I was, found, not alone anymore. The target.

BENJAMIN GASKELL (14)
Birkdale High School, Southport

THE SILENT CAVE

Water dripped from the dark, eerie cave roof as I entered its gaping mouth. Entering a pit of loneliness, I knew I would be the only one down there, alone, talking to myself. All I could see was the tiny glint of the pale moonlight behind me as I made my descent. The cave walls were completely damp, dark and decaying. The cave was completely silent, almost. I could hear the occasional scratching and sniggering ahead of me. That was when I saw it, glowing eyes and a skinny, pale body. It smirked at me. I was not alone...

MICHAEL MOSCROP (13)
Birkdale High School, Southport

THE BOY

They asked me to look after their boy for a few nights. From the minute I arrived, he was eyeing me up and down. It was as if he was studying me, finding out my greatest fears. One night, I was getting ready for bed when I heard a loud, ear-piercing shriek. I went to the boy's room, the door creaked as I opened it. I walked over to the boy. Suddenly, the door slammed shut. The boy looked up, a wide grin filled his face. He started laughing, a high-pitched cackle. I turned to go, the door was locked...

SAFWAN PATEL (13)
Birkdale High School, Southport

RED EYES

It was dark and foggy, it was pitch-black so you couldn't see a thing. There was a layer of ice upon the mud and you could see your breath. We kept slipping over and we had holes in our jackets, exposing us to the cold air. We were lost and kept going round in circles. We knew it was still behind us and we couldn't outrun it. We stopped and stared into the dark, there was nothing there. We were out of danger until we saw the scratch marks on the trees. We looked behind us. There were red eyes...

LOUIS JAMES SEARLE (12)
Birkdale High School, Southport

THE FOREST

The fog appears and the forest darkens. Out of the distant fog, a shadow emerges. The shadow leads to a slim figure and I tremble in fear. I try not to show I am terrified, but the chills it sends down my spine are unbearable. I shine my bright torch at its pale face, but it is unresponsive; it doesn't blink and its eyes light up the fog circulating us. I hope for something to break the ice, but nothing does. It just stands there staring at me from across the eerie, desolate land...

DION RIMMER (13)
Birkdale High School, Southport

UNTITLED

I was seven when it all started. I was walking home from school when I heard a scream. It was no normal scream, it was a scream of horror. I ran and ran, but I couldn't get away. Something had followed me all the way from school and I hadn't noticed. But it wasn't a person, it was a shadow. I was five minutes away from home and I heard the same scream again and again. Then I turned and the shadow was back. I could see my house but it was too late, it was my turn...

JUDE MOORE (12)
Birkdale High School, Southport

HOME INVASION

It was dark, I heard the rain pattering on my window. Suddenly, glass shattered from downstairs. Scared, I pulled my thin quilt over my head. Then I listened, the stairs creaked as whatever it was came up. Terrified, I peered over my covers. I heard its nails scrape across the wall as it slowly approached my half-open door. With a long creak, the shadow advanced, getting closer to me. Hunched over, it breathed heavily. Then I gently whispered, 'Who's there?'

OLIVER JACK CROCKETT (13)

Birkdale High School, Southport

THE GRAVEYARD

I crept through the dark, gloomy graveyard, glaring at the graves. They looked peaceful and innocent but something else caught my attention. There was a loud screech from behind me, it made me wince in fear. I was reluctant to turn around but I was too curious not to. I felt like I was being watched. My heart was racing and my head was pounding. The noise was getting louder and I realised I had to go quickly or I would die. But I was frozen to the spot with fear...

DANIEL DOHERTY (13)
Birkdale High School, Southport

A Child's True Nightmare!

The building stood in front of me, I was inclined to enter. Cautiously, I inched through the bare corridor; the onslaught just ahead beckoned me, daring me towards it. My heartbeat intensified. I saw the omniscient beings before me, lurking in the shadows, consuming dignity! A freezing hand clamped onto my shoulder. 'Go ahead.' The beast's eyes pierced through the darkness, these words emanated from its mouth: 'Your grades have dropped.'

Arran Messenger (14)
Birkdale High School, Southport

HOSPITAL

Stumbling into the abandoned hospital, I saw flickering lights and drips of blood falling on shattered tiles. I knew I wasn't alone. I walked further down the creepy corridor, I saw smashed bottles and syringes on the floor. I could hear screaming in a deep voice and heavy footsteps. They got faster and faster, as if they were running on four feet. I couldn't see properly so I decided to run. It caught up to me, then it leapt onto my back!

BRANDON FRANCE (12)
Birkdale High School, Southport

BROKEN

There is the foul smell of sulphur in the air, my front door is hanging off its hinges - something is wrong. Creeping in, I try not to make a sound. The wallpaper has been torn to shreds. I walk slowly up the stairs. The trail of destruction continues upwards, right into the creepy, old attic. Although the bolted wooden door looks untouched, when I get closer I see the claw marks. Then I hear the hissing behind me...

SAM COOPER (14)
Birkdale High School, Southport

THE CHURCH

'Is that you?' I turned. 'Argh!' I screamed. I ran out of that old, worn-out church. I turned around in a circle. Oh no, I was lost in a dark, misty forest. Out of the corner of my eye I saw a black figure, not hard to miss, approaching me from the front. I screamed.

'Liz, wake up.' Argh, phew, it was just a dream, but in the back of my mind I still thought about the church and the figure.

The next night I fell asleep and saw that figure, and he took me away. I never woke up.

KIELEY MEDLEY (12)
Fleetwood High School, Fleetwood

Mental Issues

Walking up, I felt panicky. The mental asylum stood desolate, sheathed by plants. Drawings and writing from patients covered most walls. Whilst exploring, I felt as if I was being spectated - by someone or something. Each room, filled with darkness, was personalised by inmates. I peered into each room, expecting nothing. However, a body lay in one corner. I froze, stared, completely terrified. Suddenly, its eyes opened. I ran quicker than ever. The next minute felt like thirty. I only stopped when I reached peaceful civilization.

Sixteen years later, I believe that the body is still watching me.

Garrick Coventry (12)

Fleetwood High School, Fleetwood

UNTITLED

I turned, a ghostly figure approached me, looking right into my eyes. It wasn't Tom. I screamed, turning back around and before I knew it, I was running for my life. I came across many trees and bushes, but suddenly I was standing somewhere different, somewhere I had been before. It was my old house. I thought to myself, *maybe I should have a look around.* When I looked around, more and more things became familiar. It was strange because how could I have moved places so quickly?
'Argh!' I woke up, I realised it was all a dream.

SOPHIE HANNAH REBECCA BARNETT (12)
Fleetwood High School, Fleetwood

GRAVEYARD

Lightning struck the hay barrel on the old, dry, crumbly ground of the abandoned graveyard. Rose was on her way home, she had run away earlier that day and missed her family. She'd decided to take a short cut through the graveyard, when suddenly hay set on fire around her. She had nowhere to go. A hand grabbed her ankle and pulled her into the ground. She yelled for help and tried to get out. She gave up on help, she was gone!
She was never seen again, until today. She was stronger, faster, scared of nothing and ready for anything!

NATALIE SOUTHERN (12)
Fleetwood High School, Fleetwood

THE ABANDONED HOUSE!

There was a girl, she was walking round the forest trying to find a house where her mum and dad said that they would be waiting for her. The girl heard a noise, she looked around to see if anyone was there and saw no one.

She arrived at the house, she was looking all around the huge building, trying to find her mum and dad. But they were nowhere to be seen. She went into the house and a voice started to whisper, 'We're watching you.' The door slammed, the girl started panicking, a ghost came towards her...

ANNABELLE SHARROCK (12)
Fleetwood High School, Fleetwood

THE CHURCH OF FEARS!

I wonder who it is. I turn around to see my long-lost father standing there, cold and damp. 'Dad?'
I go to hug him, he backs away and shouts, 'Run!' The lights turn on, a choir is stood hand in hand singing! I hate choirs and I hate seeing my dad cry! My grandma runs down the aisle with her lips pushed together. I back away, the lights go off, the room is silent. I feel something tingly on my back... a spider! All my fears are coming to life! I scream and brush my body, then fall quickly downwards...

BILLIE-JO FRITH (11)
Fleetwood High School, Fleetwood

THE PATH...

As they set foot onto the muddy path, they heard a strange noise... It came from the graveyard. They started walking in to find out where the noise came from, but as they took another step they were pulled into the floor. They were stuck! There was a door, as they turned the squeaky door handle, a ghost popped out at them. There was a flicker of light and *bang!* He was gone!
'Where did he go?' she wondered. They were ghouls. They would never be seen again, or known. They were... Dead... Forever.

KIRA SAN AINSCOUGH (12)
Fleetwood High School, Fleetwood

THE SOUL

I stroll to the abandoned house. I've heard rumours about this house that there is a ghost, and some of my friends told me not to go. The people who lived here had superstitions like walk on your hands to keep the ghost away. That is weird. I look around the abandoned house, there is nothing here. Then there is something behind me. I'm running away from the thing or ghost, into the wood. I can see a ghost. I can see a church, I need to sit down.
I'm on a cliff, I lose my soul...

ADAM REYNOLDS (12)
Fleetwood High School, Fleetwood

UNEXPECTED GUESTS?

John walked into the graveyard, the gravestones coal-black, scattered with cobwebs. The night littered with fog, John walked through the musty gate as silent as a mouse. Trembling, John gifted the flowers to his grandfather's grave. As he turned his back... *crash!* The gravestones clattered to the ground like dominoes. Zombies and ghosts came jumping out - John was frozen like a statue; ghosts approached him faster than a cheetah! John gave a loud yelp (although he knew it was useless). One zombie's hand touched John's shoulder as another pushed him forward. John swerved round and recognised a familiar face...

SOPHIE MALPAS (12)
Fleetwood High School, Fleetwood

GONE...

In the dead of night, I perambulated through the tenebrous woods with my sister, Molly. We observed a decrepit manor, the door was wide open. We entered the solitary building. The statue's eyes followed me everywhere I went. *Bang!* I heard a scream. She was gone. 'Molly?' No answer. As I tiptoed up the antediluvian, bloodstained staircase, I found an inanimate body lying in the ebony bathtub. It was my unimpeachable sister. A boreal breath on my insubstantial skin sent a perturbing chill down my trembling spine. I heard the cocking of a gun followed by the words: 'You're next... '

SOPHIE PROCTOR (12)
Fleetwood High School, Fleetwood

Untitled

Before two kids went home they found an abandoned house, so they went in and the door creaked open loudly. It was so dusty they couldn't see anything and because they couldn't see anything some strange figure came and got closer and closer and closer. Holly turned around and *grab,* the monster got her. The other kid called Natasha said, 'Holly, where are you?' She heard a noise from upstairs so she went quietly. She opened a door and nobody was there so she opened the cupboard door, *squeak* it went. She found her friend's dead body. Was Natasha next?

Natasha Hames Bruneel (13)
Fleetwood High School, Fleetwood

THE DARK DREAM

I was walking down the creaky stairs, stammering at each step I took. The door opened with a shriek of sadness! I slowly gazed around, jumping at every blade I saw. Was it a torture room? *Ding!* I jumped back, banging into chains and blades. The blades scraped all down my back. It was like a death room! *Bang... bang!* Suddenly, footsteps came from the hallway which led to darkness. I jumped out of my skin, I couldn't move - I was frozen! A tall, dark figure emerged from the pitch-black. Then I realised... was this the end of me?

REBECCA HALL (12)

Fleetwood High School, Fleetwood

THE FOOTPRINTS

Lightning strikes as you walk in the abandoned nursery. The door slams shut behind you as you walk along the creaky floorboards. Suddenly, the floor breaks and *bang!* you fall through. When you fall, you notice a piece of paper. You grab the paper which says, 'Leave while you still can... ' You shout to see if anyone is there, but all you hear is your voice echoing. You then jump up, look around and notice a footprint. You look at it and see there's a trail. You follow. Reaching the end of the footprints, you then see your unexpected doom...

ELISE FULLER (11)

Fleetwood High School, Fleetwood

THE POSSESSED FAMILY

It was a dark and stormy night, James was sat alone playing video games. Suddenly, he heard noises outside that he hadn't heard before. He decided to investigate. While James was outside, his mum was constantly ringing him, she wanted to know where he was. *Smash!* Rocks were falling all around him. He was stuck! He found a small opening amongst all the rocks. He was free! When he got home, he realised that all his family had been possessed. They were coming for him! He had to run. That was all he could do. He couldn't fight them...

JAMES CARTMELL (12)
Fleetwood High School, Fleetwood

THE NIGHT

Jess drove along a cold, curvy road. There were sharp twists and turns in the road. Her music was as loud as a roaring lion. The music stopped, the headlights flickered and in that split second of thinking time, she looked around. Suddenly, a tree violently fell on the road. Jess froze, the fear encased her in a bubble. She carefully exited the car, still inside her imaginary bubble. A tall, dark figure emerged from the shadows. It drew its claws and walked forwards slowly. She took a deep breath, the figure drew near, and in a split second... gone!

KAITLYN ELLA SCOTT (12)
Fleetwood High School, Fleetwood

THE GIRL WHO LOVED THE DARK

It was a windy night. The girl didn't want to go home. She found an old mental asylum. She decided to look around. The place was a mess, snapped bones were scattered on the broken tiles beneath her. The dust made her sneeze and the sound echoed through the ghostly building. As she dragged her body through the corridor, she heard a tapping noise in the distance. The girl had goosebumps, the hairs on her neck rose to their feet like an army ready for battle. Suddenly, a colossal hand grabbed her by the shoulder. The girl never returned home!

SAMIR ATIP (12)
Fleetwood High School, Fleetwood

ALONE IN THE WOODS

It was a dark, windy night. The tent was blowing loose. My friend Sally went out to secure the tent. A few minutes had gone by. Sally hadn't returned. A strange glow appeared outside the tent. Frightened, I peered out - there wasn't anything there. The light had moved further into the wood. What was it and where was Sally? I decided to follow the light. Suddenly, I heard a blood-curdling scream. A shock circulated around my body. I had to find Sally. After a while, the light led me to a dead body. Sally's dead body...

ALEX ROWE (12)
Fleetwood High School, Fleetwood

THE SUDDEN SHIVER

Shaking my hand as I opened the rusty, creaky door, something moved behind me. I got a shiver quickly running through my body. I carried on walking through the door. I walked up the old, broken stairs with my hand along the banister, sliding it along. Out of the dusty window sat a little girl. Walking along into the bedroom, I got a shiver rushing through my body again. Opening my eyes, right in front of me was a floating ghost. 'Argh!' Running back down the stairs, slamming the door and climbing over the gates, I ran for my life!

CHARLOTTE WILLIAMSON (12)

Fleetwood High School, Fleetwood

THE NIGHT BEFORE DEATH

The breeze whispered over the sound of the creaking doors, whilst screaming in the basement began. I heard it. So I went downstairs to see if Mum heard it too. Plates crashed, cutlery clattered, something swooped past the door, it drifted into the front room. The TV turned itself on, the loud noise of Countdown blurted out! I ran upstairs and there she was, a girl not much bigger than me, she was smashing the picture of me and my dad. I burst into tears. 'Don't you tell anyone I was here!' I heard as the door slammed shut...

RHIANNON AKISTER (12)
Fleetwood High School, Fleetwood

DREAMS

As I slowly opened my eyes, the beam of light from my room window blinded me. I realised where I was - I must have fallen asleep at work. I quickly stood up and grabbed my things. It was quieter than normal, no patients shouting, no nurses rushing. It was strange. The corridor's quietness, like space, was pierced as the door whispered and danger pulled me in. I never go this way! The mysterious silence made me start worrying. The sound of metal hitting the tiles pushed my body to a trail of blood. Why didn't I leave sooner... ?

LUCY BIRCH (12)

Fleetwood High School, Fleetwood

THE FOOTSTEPS

I walked slowly towards the door and went into the house. The hallway was dark and seemed to have some sort of liquid dripping from the walls. It was getting dark outside; I could hear footsteps creeping up behind me. I shivered. It was getting cold by then and it was pitch-black outside. Suddenly, there was a bang and louder footsteps followed. Slowly, I walked up to the room the noise was coming from. I knew that I wasn't alone. I walked into the room and the door slammed behind me. Immediately, I felt a hand tap my shoulder...

RACHEL PARKINSON (11)

Fleetwood High School, Fleetwood

FALLING DOWN TO DEATH

I ran towards the gates, sadly they were locked. Some sort of smoke began covering the floor - I started searching for another way out, however there wasn't one! I heard a faint scream of, 'Jake!' So I ran in that direction. Due to the fact that smoke covered the floor, I stumbled on a rock and began to fall... I realised I was falling into a pre-dug grave. I heard footsteps, I called, 'Help!' No answer followed. I felt something fall on my head, it was dirt. Raising higher and higher. Who was filling my grave in?

MILLY HOWELL (12)
Fleetwood High School, Fleetwood

YoungWriters

The Haunted Hospital

It was a dark and gloomy night while the trees were rustling and the wind was whistling. There were two children risking their poor little lives, going into the one and only haunted hospital itself. Inside was full of dead bodies in every room... The two kids packed up their gear and got ready to go on the spookiest journey of their lives. As they walked in, the first thing they saw was a staircase so they began to walk up. All you could smell was death. The staircase was creaky and it felt like someone was watching them...

Chelsea Hopkins (12)
Fleetwood High School, Fleetwood

THE NIGHT I DIED

The rain runs down my face, dampening my hair. I'm running, the girl behind me catches up. She suddenly pulls me down. I feel blood running down my body, sticking as it dries on the hairs of my leg, ripping my flesh. I turn to see the face of my nightmares, her eyes as red as blood on snow, face as pale as a dead corpse, her lips as red as blood cells. That's when I see the teeth, sharper than a butcher's knife. She leans closer, her fangs glinting off the moon's light, then darkness washes over me...

CHARMAINE MELSOM (14)
Fleetwood High School, Fleetwood

THE FACE IN THE WINDOW

One day, there was a boy called Harvey. He walked past a house that looked like it was abandoned. Since he was bored, he opened the gate and went inside the house. He started hearing strange banging noises from a certain room. He went into the room and there was a chair rocking forwards and backwards, and no one was sat in it. A few seconds later, the chair stopped rocking and Harvey felt a gush of wind fly past him. He went into the next room, he looked out of the window and saw a face next to him...

JORDAN MAYER (13)
Fleetwood High School, Fleetwood

Untitled

'Is that you?' *Bang!* I got pushed to the filthy floor. I got up and ran through the rusty door. Tom! He was sat there laughing at me then there was a massive plume of smoke. Tom was on the floor, pouring with blood. I ran and ran and ran, I started hyperventilating. I was not sure if it was a prank but it looked real. I ran to the old rusty tower. When I slowly opened the door there were two people in the corner. I ran to the top, there was a window, I decided to jump!

Andrew Fisk (12)

Fleetwood High School, Fleetwood

UNTITLED

Two people go to the forest in the middle of the night and they come across this church. They go to the rotting old door and they say, 'Shall we explore it?' They kick the door down with no fear at all. They creep in and Tom says, 'Hello?' It echoes up and down the corridors of the ugly, horrifying church. They take a step, suddenly the door closes. They are trapped. They find a flashlight, they turn it on. The crosses are on the floor, full of blood. Tom is gone, Paul faints...

PAUL HINE (13)
Fleetwood High School, Fleetwood

THE FOREST

One day, I went to the forest. It was dark and it was foggy. The fog came along, footsteps were behind me and then as I walked past, I saw a house. It was not just a house, it was a haunted house. Then I met this girl called Chelsea. We went past the haunted house and she said, 'Let's go and have a look.' The doors crept open as we went inside the enormous haunted house. Then something crept towards me, footsteps were coming towards me. I was scared, I didn't know what to do...

OLIVIA DALZELL (12)
Fleetwood High School, Fleetwood

THE FOGGY HOWL

The fog surrounds Jade with a howl following her. She runs to an abandoned house with no nice look to it. She sprints up with a crash at the door and a growl. Jade runs into an empty room with a pile of boxes. The moonlight fills the room. The beast walks in with a ghastly howl. Jade shakes as she creeps out of the room. She grabs everything she can to block the door and runs for the door downstairs. Jade runs back into the fog with the deadly howl fading away, creeping her out forever.

CAITLIN JADE WALSH (13)
Fleetwood High School, Fleetwood

UNTITLED

I slowly turned around. When I was moving, the hand started moving off my shoulder. It was Tom I think. Well, I don't know because he was wearing a mask... Yes, it was Tom and he was wearing a mask. We started heading for the door, but it was locked. I don't know why but it was bolted with about ten padlocks. We started looking for a different way out. On our way we saw blood dripping from the ceiling and a hand as a lampshade. Let's just say that we didn't make it out!

GEORGIA LOUISE BIDLE (12)

Fleetwood High School, Fleetwood

THE HAND

I shivered from the cold hand grasping my arm, getting tighter. I could smell a fire under the church. I tried to stand but the hand pushed down. I put my hand on the window ledge and pulled, and this time I got up. As I got up, the hand fell off. A hand, a full hand. But the only person who came was Tom. Was this Tom's hand? Oh, there's Tom, the hands were plastic! I picked the hand up and threw it at Tom because he was laughing at me. Then the chandelier fell on Tom, then me!

NATHAN THOMAS SHAWCROSS (12)
Fleetwood High School, Fleetwood

UNTITLED

I turned around to find out it wasn't him. I screamed for Tom, no answer. The person was staring at me with a scar on his cheek and his clothes had rips in them. I ran through the door, through the gravestones and climbed over the gate. I stopped running to look behind me and no one was there. I had lost Tom. I shouted for him again and heard a scream. Tom's voice. He shouted for me, I ran back to the creepy old church. I helped him climb over the gate and we ran away.

BELLA COATES (11)
Fleetwood High School, Fleetwood

THE WHISPERER

I was having a sleepover at my best friend's house that night. I woke up hearing my best friend calling my name from downstairs. Through the curtains I could see the moon glowing in the sky. My eyes scanned the room. My best friend was asleep in the room. I decided to sneak down and investigate. As I sauntered downstairs I felt a sudden cold draught rush past. I looked around but found nothing until I felt cold hands rest on my shoulders from behind me...

LEIGH MOUNCE (14)
Fleetwood High School, Fleetwood

Untitled

I looked behind me to see who was behind me and it didn't look like Tom at all. I screamed in fear as tears fell. I was scared and didn't know what to do. I was nowhere near the gravestones. The person was wearing a mask and was all in black. He chased me around and I finally found the graveyard. He couldn't find me so I crept behind a grave and hid behind it. Tom shouted so I ran to him and he told me it was him who was in the mask. I was relieved.

Sydney Aaiyliah Joyce (12)
Fleetwood High School, Fleetwood

THE FOREST

I strolled through the moonlit woods. It was pitch-black, I couldn't see where I was going. I got halfway and heard a lot of noises like strangers or zombies coming to attack! I was freaked out. I saw a shadow on rocks, it came closer and closer. I finally found my way out, I walked down the path. I walked past a lot of scary shops. I saw faces in the shop windows. I got home, I went to bed and saw the shadow I'd seen in the woods. I screamed...

CHELSEA STARKEY (13)
Fleetwood High School, Fleetwood

ONE WAY OUT!

The cold hand vanished, I was petrified. I looked around me and fog had slowly started to surround me. There was no way out. I sat on a dusty old tomb and it started to move. I jumped up in fear. The only way out was through the fog and it burned. I took one big breath and I ran through the fog and I bumped into Tom. We ran out the door and I told him what happened and showed him all my blisters from the burning fog. I will never ever go there again.

ANGEL MINTO (12)
Fleetwood High School, Fleetwood

UNTITLED

Tonight I'm going to meet my mate because we have researched an abandoned house. We set off at about 7:30pm and it is half an hour away. We get to the abandoned house and we hear a weird noise like screaming from a little nine-year-old girl. We go up the stairs and see a cat. I jump out of my skin. We leg it downstairs and someone is following us. We go outside and I turn back and *he* is in the top window...

JOSHUA JAMES JONES (13)
Fleetwood High School, Fleetwood

UNTITLED

I shouted. I didn't know who it was, it was really scary. I felt a cold body lying on my feet. I ran as quick as I could to the door but the door was locked. It wouldn't open. I tried to climb out of the windows but they were locked too. There was a secret door, I went down and I saw dead bodies. I tried a window again but it was locked. I heard a big bang, it was a window being smashed. I finally got out of it.

CHLOE BASTIN (12)
Fleetwood High School, Fleetwood

THE SECRET

The silent echo of the dead rippled miserably. The darkness, chilling my spine. 'Hello?' I shouted, creeping one stair at a time. The boards bowed and warned me not to go any further. The morgue below, there was a stench of rotten flesh. Laid out carefully were the scalps of poor souls, their bodies lay limp on trollies. Out of the corner of my eye, a corpse's finger twitched, I paused. In desperation I ran towards the door, I got halfway when it slammed shut. I screamed! This was it; I had been locked away for good. 'Help!'

JOEL OGDEN (14)

Ullswater Community College, Penrith

STAND OFF

John walked in the moonlit sky and then, 'Awooh!'
'What was that?' John picked up his pace, faster and faster.
Then again, 'Awooh!'
John decided to go through the woods as it would be
quicker but... *scamper, scamper, scamper.* He knew
somebody, or something, was behind him. Then he stopped
and out of the corner of his eye this thing was running at
him. *Whoosh!* Over him the beast flew. It came back for
another go. The beast ran up and jumped on him. John tried
to stop it, but no. 'Sweet payback!' shouted the beast.

BEN PERRIS (12)
Ullswater Community College, Penrith

CHURCH SURPRISE

It was coming. Where to go? I was all alone. 'Holly?' There was no answer. Had it got her?
In the corner of my eye I saw a church. It was the safest place in the whole world. But would it keep the fog out? I ran as I got closer it seemed to be telling me not to go inside. But I did. The door opened. I went in. I heard a noise. I saw Holly.
'Where were you?'
A monster was behind her - I screamed. Was this my final hour? The fog wasn't the problem now...

SAVANNAH EDWARDS-LYNCH (13)

Ullswater Community College, Penrith

MIDNIGHT PANIC

I step lightly towards the dark, dusty door. Every step I take I feel more anxious. *Creak!* I open the door. Strong winds blow towards me. Midnight strikes on the clock at the end of the hall. All of a sudden, I hear a voice.

'Hello?' I say. 'Is anyone there?' The voice calls again. I start to panic. What shall I do?

Blood starts to drip from the damp, mouldy roof. I take one step towards the stairs and I can feel my spine tingle...

NATHAN JACK LEE (12)

Ullswater Community College, Penrith

DARKNESS

Something stealthily creeps, *thud!* The beating heart, *slap!* The feet below, veins are pulsing, heart racing... Breath upon, the footsteps backwards near the edge... 'Boo!' You turn startled, but slip. Your brother is cackling, pulling a mask off, you fall to your doom... *Splash!*
Suddenly, in icy-cold water the current carries you downstream. You know it's over, you assume the cold torment will be gone but you have never passed. You emerge from the raging torrent, on soft ground. 'Heaven?' Your first question. You open your eyes, you're on soft grass. A warm breeze is caressing your face. It's over...

ELEANOR JANE FARTHING (12)
Ullswater Community College, Penrith

The Puppet Maker

It was dark, everyone in form was quiet, they were all looking at him, so was I. *Ring!* Everybody jumped, it was the bell. He left first. I decided to follow him. He went a way I'd never been down before, there was a little light in the hallway. I followed him and I heard him talk.

'Hello there my lovelies,' he said in the weirdest tone. I broke into a smile. I thought, *he's insane, there's nobody down there.* Suddenly I thought differently, *maybe there is but I won't know unless I check.* I looked and screamed. Polyester humans!

Ben Sharpe (13)
Ullswater Community College, Penrith

Behind You!

He crept to the decrepit door. Only, the crickets could be heard, repeating their scary tune. Ruined, the house stood out in the spooky woods. Over the path he crept, every time he stepped ringing could be heard. He pushed the door open and was welcomed by a loud creak. He slowly stepped into the decaying house. Local stories told the horrors of this house. Haunted by ghosts who couldn't get out. Murders happened there that couldn't be forgotten. He tiptoed into the living room. He had a hard, long stare in the mirror. A terrifying figure was behind him...

James Jones (12)

Ullswater Community College, Penrith

HONOUR MAN

You creep down the road in darkness and see an abandoned church in the way. Deciding to walk down the church, you open the door. You hear a scream and look behind you. There is nothing there so you venture forwards, up the stairs where you see a light coming from one of the rooms. Creeping forwards, you open the door. With a flash, a ghost flies at you, screaming, 'Go away!'
This doesn't stop you. Thunder and lightning strike and light up the shadows of trees. Something then touches your shoulder. You scream, 'Help! I'm too young to die!'...

BEN THOMPSON (14)
Ullswater Community College, Penrith

IT

Dark, quiet, the clock tolls 12 and black paints the sky. Nobody knows where it hides. I see the speckled light; report is back; my senses are down. *Bang!* In front it feels me move. Just down the hall and to the left is where my bed lies. 'I can't see!' Its silhouette stands, it watches from down the hall. It pounces on me... or in me. I stop, blink, listen. It wasn't me walking, it was a ghostly twin covered in bloody chains. I run back to my bed where she lies, man and moon grinning moonlight.
'My eyes!'

FERN DENNEY (13)
Ullswater Community College, Penrith

Trick Or Treat?

It was Halloween. We were going to the old house. I went at midnight. I was early. It was quiet, there was nothing around. Maybe they weren't coming. Maybe they'd set me up?

Suddenly I heard something. It kept coming closer. I ran. My phone ran out - I couldn't do anything. I heard a voice, 'Trick or treat?' It chased me all the way to the school. There was another voice, 'Come join us.' All the doors shut. *Bang!* There was a girl in the middle of the room. She didn't move. I felt a hand on my shoulder...

Kacper Zbikowski (13)
Ullswater Community College, Penrith

THE GIRL...

He stepped lightly across the wooden floorboards towards the stairs, there was an eerie silence throughout the house. Suddenly, he heard a loud, blood-curdling scream. 'Hello?' he shouted. No reply. He continued to walk up the stairs and into the room on the left. It was a bedroom. He walked to the window and looked out, in the garden he saw her staring at him. He backed away from the window, then he felt a draught of cold air brush past his face. A soft voice whispered, 'Hi.' He turned around to see her reaching for him...

LAUREN ADAMS (13)
Ullswater Community College, Penrith

MYSTERIOUS STORM

Lying awake, I couldn't sleep. There was a storm. Crashing came from outside and rain hit the windows. Darkness surrounded me as flashes of lightning lit up my room. As night carried on, noises came from downstairs, I could hear the stairs creaking. Slowly, I crept out of my room. I only had a torch and I could see a little girl dressed in a pink dusty dress. Eyes white, mouth stitched together, she was possessed. I ran back to my bed and hid. Hopefully, she wouldn't find me. But it was too late.
'Help me! Help me!'

CHLOE EARL (14)
Ullswater Community College, Penrith

THE HOUSE

I head towards the door of the crooked house. As I open the door, there is a cold chill down my spine. I know something is wrong but I make my first step into the house. *Bang!* The door slams behind me. A rush of adrenaline floods me, I sprint up the stairs and with every step I take it feels like someone is following me.

'Hello? Is anyone there?' I screech. A strong wind blows through the whole house, the shutters bang loudly, burning my ears. It all suddenly stops. I turn around - she is standing there!

KATE HORNBY (12)

Ullswater Community College, Penrith

Locked In The Bedroom

This is a dangerous part of the town. People don't last very long here. This is Pategill.

A young boy named Christian walked briskly to his friend Josh's house. He heard footsteps behind him and turned around, there was no one there. He reached Josh's house. He knocked, there was no answer. Josh appeared behind him. Josh pushed him through the door. The inside of the house was dark. Josh took Christian upstairs and locked him in the bedroom. No one knows what happened to Christian except Josh.

Ben Devlin (14)

Ullswater Community College, Penrith

THE WOLF IN SHEEP'S CLOTHING

There was thick, humid fog as far as the eye could see. I'd lost my friend. I was tired from running. I escaped the Morpher. I didn't think Harry had made it. A misty figure appeared ahead. It was Harry, he was holding something. It was sharp! Then I remembered. Oh no - the Morpher! I blinked and he was gone. I ran. I looked behind me. It was there. I shouted, 'Leave me alone!' It ran after me. I blacked out.

When awoke a knife was in my hand and I was pinned down. I was not escaping this...

CHARLIE KIRKLAND (13)

Ullswater Community College, Penrith

ALONE

Jake said he would look after me when Mum and Dad left. However, as soon as they were gone, he was gone too. Now I lie in my bed on my own in the dark with only the silence to accompany me. As I wriggle from side to side in my bed, my doll falls out. Slowly I reach my hand out from my bed. I feel the fluffy velvet carpet, but no doll. Quickly, I pull my hand back under the covers. My heartbeat speeds up rapidly. Gradually, I hear the front door creak open. I'm not alone...

'Help!'

ELLIE LLOYDS (11)
Ullswater Community College, Penrith

THE HAUNTED NIGHT

Bang! A loud bang came from the house next door. They were strange, the people next door, they weren't, well... well I guess they weren't normal. *Bang!* Another. What was it? I found myself slowly climbing the rotten fence that cut through our gardens. A bird flew through the window so I followed. I entered through the open window. I made my way down the gloomy hallway. I heard creaking ahead, slowly making its way near, picking up pace... A cold breeze then touched my hand...

HUGH BURNE (14)

Ullswater Community College, Penrith

Haunted Hotel

I really don't know what we were thinking... That night when you sleep at your friend's house and you want to act cool. He lives next to an abandoned hotel. He dares you to go in and you do it, you enter the hotel, your friend follows behind you. You hear footsteps, and you're trying to act cool. You stay in the hotel and your friend has run off, you go up to the next floor, you get the whole thing on your trusty GoPro. Then *smash! Thud!* Screams echo.
'Nooo!'

Joseph Thomas Gate (13)
Ullswater Community College, Penrith

THE DEEP DARK

It was dark night, I was on my own. I lost my group. All on my own in the forest, just my phone, nothing else. Suddenly I thought I could call my friend Jack. So I dialled his number and called him. He never answered. The phone said, 'Please leave a message.' I said, 'Hi, I'm lost. Can you come find me?' I walked on then I got a text, it said: 'I'm coming for you!' I stood still. I heard a noise and I thought it was Jack.
'Jack, is that you? Argh!'

ARTHUR BOWMAN (12)
Ullswater Community College, Penrith

Blood!

Down by the river there's an old water tunnel, just big enough for a person. It has not been used for years. All of a sudden, blood comes rushing through and the limbs from a cow flow down after it. I call the police and they check the pipe but nothing is found. I lie to myself about it. I go to shower and turn it on. Blood sprays out. I run downstairs to get Dad. We run upstairs and as I get closer the sound changes, it is just water.
The next day Mum's out and the walls bleed.

Taylor Teasdale (12)

Ullswater Community College, Penrith

THE HOUSE

This house was terrifying. It was surrounded by trees and the sun would never shine on it. According to my parents, if you got too close the spirit would latch onto you and feed off your family. There was a boy called Jack who was dared to go into the house, 3 days later he disappeared. People said he'd moved away but I knew that wasn't the case. My friend said he saw the spirit, I knew he was doing this to scare me. Days later he was gone, never to be seen again...

NAOMI PURDHAM (14)

Ullswater Community College, Penrith

WHAT WAS IT?

As I looked into the dusty, unkept mirror, I saw the abandoned old room behind me. I looked back, however I felt something drift in front of me. I looked back. Who was it? What was it? I uncomfortably walked out of the spooky house. The mist was blocking my way so I couldn't see. Something grabbed me. I reached out and rubbed my back nervously...

I have always looked back at that day and wondered who or what it was!

ROMNEY THOMPSON (12)

Ullswater Community College, Penrith

THE TEXT MESSAGE

I turned the handle, the door creaked open. 'Hello?' No reply, silence. My trembling body crept inside. I heard my phone beep twice, but I didn't answer. A vast staircase lay ahead of me, whispers echoing through my ears. *Bang!* I fell to the floor. By now I couldn't reach my phone. My heart was beating 10 times faster than normal. Looking up, in shock I saw the words: 'Next time answer the text', imprinted in the roof. I stood up shaking. 'Help!' I ran down the staircase, through the hallway and opened the door. I couldn't believe my eyes...

HOLLY GATE (12)

Ullswater Community College, Penrith

Spooky, Scary Skeletons

Footsteps coming towards him. He couldn't breathe, suffocating, unstable, disorientated, he stepped hastily to the decrepit door. Panicking, he turned the handle. Nothing. He banged his head on the door. The door knocked back. In confusion and fright, he stumbled backwards into another room. He hit the curtain and heard crunching. He held his breath as he felt and saw a rotting, decaying hand on top of his hand and one on his mouth. It snapped his neck. He fell to the ground as the skeletons began feasting on his flesh and blood squirted everywhere. Death was slow and agonising.

Edward Greed (12)
Ullswater Community College, Penrith

Lucy's Luck

It was her first time on the spaceship. Lucy was worried inside though, she would be tied to a rope, for safety, but it terrified her. She ignored the good luck. Stepping onto the new planet was breathtaking. Her space boots brushed the dusty ground slowly, to the applause of her team. 'See, no aliens!' she whispered to herself. She felt fine until she lost contact with the group, completely distressed. But when the signal regained, and Lucy was shown strangled, the team were in shock. The words written in blood made it even worse: 'Aliens can kill too!'

Lilly Nulty (11)

Ullswater Community College, Penrith

Terror Town

Darkness fell upon the old abandoned town; the wind picked up and beckoned furiously. Across the ground was smashed glass and dirty litter that crunched like bones in the monstrous breeze... Suddenly, the sound of footsteps grew gradually louder - they were moving at a strangely fast pace, as an old street lamp flickered vigorously; a glimpse of her pale face, flushed cheeks and golden locks was caught. Panting heavily, she paused for one single moment then broke out in a run once again. As fast as lightning, chills flew through my body in fear... What was she running from?

Eve Edmondson (14)
Ullswater Community College, Penrith

DEATH AROUND THE CORNER...

I'd heard rumours about his place. But were they true? Who knows? It was a terrible day. I know it was just a dare, but I'd be hated for life if I didn't do it. We were walking in the woods when Marci dared me to enter the old, crooked house. So I said, 'Yeah alright.' Unaware of the dangers within. It was just one small step. The door creaked slowly as a cave-like scene appeared through the fog. 'Marci?' The door shut. Locked. A cold, icy feeling arose as a white hand was presented. 'Help Marci!' Silence followed...

SARAH HALE (13)
Ullswater Community College, Penrith

THE HOUSE

Empty. Everywhere you looked it was empty. But at exactly one in the morning you saw it. It towered above you. Its bricks crumbled as you touched them. What you saw was a house that must have been abandoned years ago. The door was like the entrance to a cave; it spookily beckoned you inside. However, as you entered you instantly regretted it, as the door disappeared, leaving you inside forever. As you explored the house you saw nothing but hallways. Then you realised there's only a certain amount of time until sunrise, when the house would disappear with you...

LOUIE BELLAS (15)
Ullswater Community College, Penrith

The Missing

The castle stood silent as always. No one dared to venture through the opposing gates that led to the castle. Everyone had their own theories; no one dared even whisper them. Those who did were either brave or stupid, and would often disappear! No matter how many people looked, the missing people were never found. Sometimes the searchers would tell tales of blood-curdling screams and the pleas for help. When they looked closer, there was nothing. Only a breath of wind moving the trees. The people who heard these tales would be forever haunted by screams and pleas.

Anna Dinsdale (14)

Ullswater Community College, Penrith

DESPAIR

Tha-thud! The once eternal silence that fell over the school - broken! A breath, a shriek, then anguish. A sheet of rage and sorrow draped over the ultimate biker's mind. The weapon fell to the floor with a thud. This was a homicide. There would be a class trial, and if anyone found out... No, they wouldn't. After all, he had his 'brother'. All he had to do was pin it on her. Everyone hated her anyway. But as the poor man found out... wishes don't come true. Round and around. The bike span. Bye Mondo. Now corpse-paste. And despair!

NICOLE BAILEY (11)

Ullswater Community College, Penrith

THE HAUNTING

My breath became heavier the faster I ran. I could feel my heart pounding out of my chest. The demonic demon grew closer, edging ever closer. I could feel its freezing cold soul, sending shivers up my spine and goosebumps on my trembling arms. I couldn't dare look behind. My footsteps sent tremors into the rotten floorboards. I slammed the door behind me. The sound of silence grew louder, as I watched the door, terrified of what would come. Suddenly, a strange noise came from the wardrobe. Investigating seemed risky but I had to know what was inside...

RYAN MOLE (14)
Ullswater Community College, Penrith

THE HAUNTED HOUSE

It was a dark, gloomy night, a young girl and her friends were walking through a spooky forest. They came across an old spooky house. They walked towards the house and cautiously pushed the wooden door open - sitting in front of them was an old, creepy china doll, swaying from side to side. The four girls were absolutely terrified, two of them went back home. The young girl went through the door and hanging above her was a huge spider. Her best friend moved slowly backwards and the next thing she heard was her friend scream. She was gone.

EMMA NOBLE (13)
Ullswater Community College, Penrith

Forgotten Time

A tear fell down her cheek. As her faint cry escaped her lips, she placed a beautiful rose on the gravestone. Curious, I approached her. The heavy snow cascading down on her. Fog, dancing down on the moss-infested graves. Under the dark, her wet and bedraggled face was unrecognisable. Gently, I placed my hand on her shoulder: she didn't move. 'Are you okay?' I asked... No reply. Glancing at the stone I read a familiar name. My name! Baffled, I looked around me. The snow on the ground was a clear blanket, my footsteps nowhere to be seen...

Carys Benn (13)

Ullswater Community College, Penrith

WATCH YOUR BACK

I walked up to the old school stairs, they were worn-down concrete. There were oak wood banisters going down the long staircase. It was dark and gloomy and mist crept under the wooden door. I was on my own. Suddenly, there was a whisper, 'Watch your back, watch your back, watch your back!' Strange, nobody ever came down here! I ran up the stairs and through the door. Pictures! There were pictures all over the wall! I slowly walked across the room. I was alone. At least I thought I was. There was a tap on my shoulder... 'Argh!'

FRASER LITTLE (12)
Ullswater Community College, Penrith

QUESTIONS OF THE SCREAMS

Anxiously, I tiptoed down the dark abandoned corridor. The stench of rotten flesh hit me, like a punch in the face. The hospital creaked as I stood shuddering against the damp cold wall. Suddenly, there was a screech coming from a distant corridor. I froze. Still as a statue. My heart was beating fast like a drum. The disgusting aroma made me feel nauseous. Questions started rushing through my head. Who was out there? What was out there? What did they want? Was I going to make it out alive? Then the screams got louder, and closer...

ALICE BAYLIFFE (15)

Ullswater Community College, Penrith

Pokémon

One cold, dark night, there was a boy called Kieron, he was walking home after a hard day of Pokémon hunting, that's when he saw a Pokémon in the house beside him. The house was boarded up with vines creeping up it, the lights were flickering but he slowly went into the ancient house. He was breathing heavily, Kieron could feel a pair of eyes staring down at him, he didn't care, the game was more important. He stepped one foot into the house, a man grabbed him. That was the last time anyone saw the little boy.

Daniel Monkhouse (14)

Ullswater Community College, Penrith

Darkness Flows Through

My limp subject awoke, confused as predicted, but eerily
silent. He was quiet, as was the darkness surrounding him.
The microphone picked up only the presence of darkness,
the crackle of death. Until he let out his most blood-curdling
cry. The syringe broke the fragile skin and I repeated
'76275'. Recognition entered his eyes, he knew the code. I
repeated the message and told him to describe it, no
response. Had I pushed him too far? Was the process
started too early? His time was up, we had others in
suspense, so darkness went in.

Lennox Rylands (15)

Ullswater Community College, Penrith

CLOSER

As the mysterious fog gathered it got colder and darker. I could see frightening dark figures getting closer as I walked to the abandoned house. They started to come from all directions. I sprinted as fast as I could to the house, breathlessly. I entered the house, the floorboards creaked. It sounded like a little girl screaming. As I walked up the creaking stairs the door slammed! Someone was in this house with me! I was scared, my heart was beating as fast as a hyena running. Suddenly, a quiet voice behind me said, 'It was you!'

DYLAN LOURIE (14)
Ullswater Community College, Penrith

THE ALARM CLOCK

The last thing I saw was my alarm clock flashing 12:07 before she pushed her long, rotting nails through my chest, her other dry crackly hand muffling my screams, I sat bolt upright relieved it was only a petrifying, blood-curdling dream. But as my alarm clock read 12:06 I heard my closet door slowly creak open. My eyes widened as I slowly pulled the soft heavy sheets to my tense ears and quieted my breathing until I realised I could hear calm, heavy breathing but my breath was held. That silent drum driving my body got violently faster.

ROWAN MCCARTHY (15)

Ullswater Community College, Penrith

THE PURPLE VICTIMS

Stretching far and wide, in all colours, shapes and sizes lay the victims. Their skin, bruised and battered, was purple in colour. I could hear them scream out to me as the large blade sheared off their hanging limbs. Then it began, it smelt like rotting flesh and the repetitive noise in my head began to grow louder. Questions were going through my mind. Could I help them? Should I leave them be? Suddenly, without thinking, I lashed out at them like a cheetah and grabbed them by their necks. In the bin they went. No more fruit left now!

CRAIG BOTTOMLEY (14)
Ullswater Community College, Penrith

EYES

The cringing squeak of the gate in the eerie silence. Gusts of wind rustled the undergrowth of the neglected garden. Blankets of fog covered the gnawing teeth from the crumbling bricks that were hanging off the old lady's hideout. The door was rotten and it was as if it were trying to keep all people out. The rusty hinges suddenly jolted and the door flew open. Smelling the musty air caused a bony hand to squeeze my lungs. Large beetle families scuttled across the dusty hearth in the long hallway. Eyes looking at me, I sensed it...

FREYA WESTON (14)

Ullswater Community College, Penrith

GHOSTLY CHURCH

One lovely morning, I went outside to go to the park. I stumbled on a piece of glass, I looked up and saw a beautiful church. I went inside to explore. I found lots of broken glass and wood scattered along the floor. I shouted, 'Hello!' No answer. I went in the father's room and saw blood, medicine tablets and knives. I went around the bed and lifted up the duvet and saw bones. I was really scared. Suddenly, I heard the doors slam shut. I went to the toilets and saw on the mirror: 'I will find you'.

RYAN EVELEIGH (12)
Ullswater Community College, Penrith

III

WHAT LURKS BELOW

There was an old abandoned church, walking towards the veranda, the door swung open, pulling me inside. The clock struck two and the fog rolled in through the windows and the front door. There was a bang. Lightning struck and the rain came pouring through the holes in the roof. I ran to the basement using only the light on my phone. The stairs creaked as I walked. The door slammed shut behind me. It was freezing. There were old metal bars on the windows with no way out. There was an old rotting coffin. Should I have opened it?

ROXANNE HODGSON (14)

Ullswater Community College, Penrith

DARK DEPTHS

In the dark depths of the Mongolian dungeons I walked
through. Water pounded down on the concrete floor. I was
trying not to slip over. I swam through black, dirty sewage -
it was like swimming through solid ice. Cobwebs hung
down. Snakes slithered. I was scared! I climbed up a ladder
and pulled the drain lid from above me. I saw something. I
could see a huge shadow. It had thick grey fur. I could hear
it quietly groaning. I saw its huge hands and feet. It was
eating something. It smelt rotten, I thought it was a person.

MATTHEW WILLS (15)
Ullswater Community College, Penrith

RAVEN...

The playground was empty as I walked through. 'Don't enter!' screeched a raven sitting on the bell. I went in anyway and looked around, the smell of must hitting my face. All I could hear was the sound of my shoes on the stone floor. I looked down, blood was all I saw. The cold iron doorknob squealed as I turned it. Nothing! I turned but as I did the ear-clenching screech of fingernails running down the blackboard startled me. At that moment I realised I definitely wasn't alone and I needed to get out right now!

LAUREN CARIS (12)
Ullswater Community College, Penrith

THE CELLAR

Cautiously tiptoeing down the cold staircase, the alleyway emerges into a damp cold cellar. Bats skim my head with their wings. The cellar door slams behind me as I jump. I hear other footsteps as I slowly tune in to the sounds of the cellar. I begin sweating as salty water sprints down my face. I close my eyes in fear, hoping it's a dream. The sweet smell of blood pirouettes up my nose. I turn around. I wish I hadn't. A man stands in front of me, knife in hand. I scream, 'Help me!' but it's too late.

ISABELLE BOOTHMAN (12)
Ullswater Community College, Penrith

THE STORY OF BROOKSIDE MANOR

Walking ever so slowly down into the abandoned manor house, my entire body shook. I placed my hand on the door handle, which felt like water itself, and with huge amounts of hesitation, I turned it and stepped in. The hairs on the back of my neck stood up as if they knew something was wrong. Cautiously creeping forward down the elongated hallway, I turned my head to the left and noticed a shadow moving to the door's window. Suddenly, I heard the loudest shriek of horror. I peered into the window again and I was horrified!

HOLLY WILMOT (15)

Ullswater Community College, Penrith

THE GIRL WHO NEVER LIVED

I'm falling into the deep, dark depths of Hell. Chasms of fire. Screams of nothing. I'm here, Hell-hounds have found me. They tear me to shreds. They leave me for dead but I'm alive. I'm a pile of bones. A ghost. How will I survive? I turn to see hieroglyphics telling me all I can eat is flesh and souls. I will train the Hell-hounds to tear apart every human heart, in the world, if it's the last thing I do. My first victim will be my friend, so she can feel my pain. Beware, beware, I'm coming for you!

GABRIELLE JANE BAILEY (13)
Ullswater Community College, Penrith

RUN

The darkness surrounded me. I was alone, hungry; fighting for my life. I could feel a warm breath tingle down my spine. I ran. Voices echoed around me and in my head. It had been three days. I needed to get out. There was a crack in the door and a ray of light came rushing in. The darkness was finally clear. The grimy cobweb-riddled room had a window. Thoughts gushed into my head: *I'm going to live!* I cautiously stepped closer to the window. Pain took over my body. Then I heard the noise I had been dreading...

MOLLY COWARD (14)
Ullswater Community College, Penrith

The Forgiving Light

Bellowing; the wind funnelled through the skeleton forest. *Clash!* I opened the frozen gate. I saw a beckoning light in the distance. My feet fell in front of each other. Mercilessly, the rain fell; nearly there. I lurched forward into the forgiving light. There, in the centre of the shack, lay a tiny bowl of tranquil water. I gazed over to see an unrecognisable blood-covered face. Trembling, I backed away, into the icy air. I turned around. My scream surged out like a wave. I fell to the floor completely lifeless.

Kelly Noble (14)

Ullswater Community College, Penrith

The Run

The mysterious fog crawled across the meadows like demons crawling out of Hell. I had to hide, there was a building in the trees. I couldn't make out what type. I went to the window, my reflection all I could see. I blinked, it was there. It screamed a distinct noise, it brings shivers to my spine even today! I stumbled back in horror and went into a flat spin, wondering what had happened. 'What was that?' I ran to see what was there and there was nothing. I ran as fast as anything, back to the safety of town.

Arran Barber (14)

Ullswater Community College, Penrith

Josh's Story

One night, there was a boy called Josh roaming the streets of Paingill, looking for his parents who had strangely gone missing. The night was dark and the air was cold. There lay a blanket of mist on the frozen soil. Josh went down an alley to get to his house but there stood a black figure at the end. He was waiting and watching Josh. Josh was scared but carried on down the alley. He grabbed Josh and pulled him in. Josh couldn't move. The man was breathing heavily. Josh was terrified. Josh knew there was no escape...

Tyson Weir (14)
Ullswater Community College, Penrith

WOKEN DEAD

The oak door opened; a draught engulfed the house. Small white hands released their grip on the brass knob, the floor creaked and cracked as she entered. Of course Lola Rodney, the smallest girl in school, dared to enter. Her face went blue and her eyes dulled as the moon was no more. Walking around, she felt as if the house was watching her, as if the dead had just woken. Her mind went blank, her heart pumped faster. A silk veil cloaked her. She walked outside to meet the bullies. That was the last anyone heard of them.

ELIZABETH JACKSON (11)
Ullswater Community College, Penrith

GLOOMY GLANCE

Fog was creeping over, we shivered through the forest. Suddenly, we saw a still building. We turned towards the building. A blood-curdling scream shot through me. We walked to the rusty gate. I shivered and mumbled, 'Should we be in here?' I turned, she had gone. What should I do now? I went to the rotten stairs, they creaked. Somebody was behind me, I could hear them. I still walked on. I glanced over, there was a bloody body. I felt a hand on my shoulder... Was I next? What should I do now? Oh no, it was over!

CHARLIE FELTON (12)
Ullswater Community College, Penrith

THE MINERS

I hammered away like I always do. I knew there had been a caving in and lots of people died, but *that* was ages ago. I was hammering at this rock, when I came upon a skull. I froze. I watched it for a moment, then ran! I could not think straight, the skull had smiled. I looked around and saw a ghost. It was attacking my friends and turning *them* into ghosts. I sprinted this time. I had to get out. I had to warn people. I suddenly stopped. Something had touched me. I looked up and screamed, 'No!'

ISABELLE LEONARD (12)
Ullswater Community College, Penrith

13

A snowflake fell. It gently skimmed my face. I turned my head to see it fall and that was when I saw it. Rusting away, a sign with the number 13 fell off the door, into the snow. I stepped back, then I heard footsteps from inside. I wasn't the only one that had survived. Peering up at the window, I saw a child weeping. Then it went silent. The whole forest went silent. I was being watched from the window. I looked up again, she was gone. My heart started beating loudly. Something grabbed me. I was gone.

NIAMH BRENAN (12)

Ullswater Community College, Penrith

THEN THERE WERE NONE

The poem starts with nine, then there were none. Nine kids walking slowly along the beach sat down and told this story. Jack was so scared he walked away and never returned. Ben went to look for Jack but didn't come back. Two kids went into the sea, they drowned straight away when one broke their knee. Lily ran and fell and died. This story was coming true! In a few minutes they went from four to two. Lauren jumped off a wall, broke her neck and was gone. The last one gave a scream and then there were none!

SAMANTHA WESTGARTH (12)

Ullswater Community College, Penrith

DOLL

With a shaking hand Maya opened the creaking door. A musty smell filled her nostrils. It looked like she was in a hall. All Maya could see was a wooden staircase. Silently, she slipped upstairs. The place looked dusty and forgotten. The moon was rising and mist fell. Where should she go now? *Creak!* Maya gasped, something was coming towards her, she could hear it. Maya saw what it was. A doll! Thread was through its mouth, its eyes were lifeless. Maya was trapped. She shut her eyes and prayed for help.

RUBY EDEN (12)
Ullswater Community College, Penrith

THE MANOR

Midnight... My torchlight trembled as my hand began to shudder. An eerie mist crept in below my feet and weaved between the gaps in the spiked metal gate. The hinge screeched open and I began to approach the abandoned manor. The rotting door was covered in a repugnant green substance that I dared to touch; turning the handle my heart began to pound harder and faster for each anxious step I took. *Creak! Squeak...* What was that? Could it be a mouse? No! A bitter breeze made my neck hair stand on end...

ROSIE HORNE (14)

Ullswater Community College, Penrith

Shadows

How could something so beautiful be so creepy? I thought, walking through the woods. As I walked, the shadows caught up with me. I got the feeling of being watched. The feeling of being followed. A cold draught of air slithered down my spine. Frozen in horror, my feet glued to the floor in terror. Something was there. I was not alone. A blood-curdling scream came from a high-branched tree. I looked up and saw a woman. She had blood trickling down from her slit throat. She was swinging from a coil of rope.

Teri Ann Chadwick-Whalley (13)

Ullswater Community College, Penrith

WHEN I WOKE UP DEAD!

I sprang to life with a dead face covered in blood. All I remembered was a sharp pain through the spine then black. I met a girl earlier that night, she was quite strange, wearing a cloak that was torn and dirty. I took her as a cos-player. She was saying, 'I'm a necromancer,' and other crazy stuff. I took it as nothing, little did I know... There was a spree of murders lately, so when I heard a woman scream close to me I ran... Then black... Now I'm up she is standing right in front of me. Help!

NATHAN SAVAGE (15)
Ullswater Community College, Penrith

ROCKING CHAIR

The door slammed as I sprinted in the other direction. I stopped instantly and slowly crept around to see the moonlit hallway leading to a pitch-black room. I walked closer. All I could feel was a cold breeze, getting colder as I got closer. I got to the door and I could hear a squeaky, creepy sound. My mind wanted to walk in but I couldn't bring my legs to walk. I did it, I was in. I turned the light on. A black figure disappeared and the rocking chair started rocking. Voices started shouting my name...

CHARLIE GRACE HEALEY (13)
Ullswater Community College, Penrith

THE UNKNOWN

On an eerily quiet night I was lying in bed unable to sleep. I heard a door creaking downstairs. I grabbed my torch and made my way down the creepy old stairs. By now, for sure, whatever it was knew I was there, I walked into the kitchen where there was a disgusting-looking human creature with parts of flesh ripped off which was hanging off its face. It looked at me, snapping its teeth. I knew the time had come where the walking dead was a thing. I ran as it sprinted after me, then it all went black...

ADAM WALTON (15)

Ullswater Community College, Penrith

Spider Killers

'John,' I shouted. 'Come over here, look what I found.' We opened the cupboard in the wall and thousands of sticky spiderwebs clung to the wall. We both grabbed a wrecked brush and brushed away the webs. We kept sweeping and sweeping until there was nothing. It seemed we had found a tunnel. We were on our hands and knees and we found a key. The key led to a door at the side. We opened the door and, woah, we fell in. All you could hear was, 'Argh!' We fell into killer spiders.

Sinead Thompson (12)
Ullswater Community College, Penrith

THE DROPPING DEAD

I woke up one drizzly morning thinking that it would be a regular Tuesday. I was wrong! I opened my curtains to see what looked like a person zoom past the window. I rushed downstairs and flung the door open to see a rotting corpse lying in front of me. I slammed the door shut and ran upstairs. I flew back into bed. After half an hour I got up again and went outside, stepped over the corpse and set off to the shops. I was about halfway when another corpse dropped across the road. Then, one hit me...

DAN HARRISON (15)

Ullswater Community College, Penrith

I Walked In The Woods

I walked and walked forever. It was like a dream, the sun and the trees. 'It's a wonderful paradise!' Then the scenery changed, the trees were closer and tighter. I heard a twig snap. I spun around and saw a blur of black stretched across my vision and then another blur. I realised I was standing on a stone grave and it had my name on it. My mobile phone rang, I answered but only static answered. A blur stopped and walked up behind me. It whispered to me, then it started to scream!

Travis Thomas Hutchcroft (12)

Ullswater Community College, Penrith

I'm Behind You!

As I walked through the forest I saw a big mansion. I knocked on the door, it opened. I stepped inside and the door slammed. I walked up the rotten staircase and I felt someone touch me. I turned slowly, no one was there! I carried on and got to a room, it said: 'Jack's room'. I walked in, there was a ghost boy carrying a knife. He walked towards me. I went towards the bed then he jumped over the dusty bed. He disappeared then I heard someone say, 'I'm behind you... '

Elenna Bullock (12)

Ullswater Community College, Penrith

I Couldn't Believe It

The trees that towered above me made me feel sick and dizzy when I looked up at them. The flowing mist scattered across the woods made it impossible to see. Howling wolves whistled in the wind. Footsteps were nearing; they were coming from all directions. I felt as though I was about to pass out. The atmosphere was overriding and possessing my body. I was paralysed from head to toe. Suddenly, shadows started to rise up my body, blocking the shining moon beams. I couldn't believe it...

Kieron Lee Phillips-Craig (14)
Ullswater Community College, Penrith

ASYLUM

The door creaked. I knew who it was. Darkness filled the room. I wasn't going to open the door as I wanted my last few seconds of freedom. I sat in the corner thinking of my past. Unsure why, as I was going to forget everything later. The door slammed and I was pushed to the ground. A sharp sting hit my neck and I was hit across the head by a bat. Everything went blurry. Once I got my vision back I was tied to a chair with blood trickling down from my head. I knew where I was...

HANNAH EMMERSON (12)

Ullswater Community College, Penrith

THE DARKNESS

I swung open the door with my crowbar and walked in. The smell of burning cigar ends overwhelmed my lungs as I stepped up the staircase and pushed down the door. I looked around and saw a large figure looming terrifyingly in the corner of the room. He wore a tweed jacket, a leather flat cap and a small Yorkshire terrier sat beside him. I glared at him as he ran at me. I got across the road and watched back in pure fear. He kept watching as I went home. I went to sleep then I saw him...

DARCY C C LEE (12)

Ullswater Community College, Penrith

Circus Nightmare

The buzz of the circus engulfed every sense of my body. The smell of candyfloss and popcorn filled me with excitement. I took my dark red seat on the very front row. Suddenly, the lights went off, I couldn't see a single thing. They started flickering. The clown's cackle and the his heavy footsteps crept up behind me. I stood still. Suddenly, a large hand grabbed my shoulders, pushing me down to the floor. I turned around, full of fear. I was helpless, this was the end...

Charlotte Holliday (14)

Ullswater Community College, Penrith

THE NIGHT OF THE FALSE STAR

I tossed and turned, tears pouring down my cheeks, my breathing rapid. It was the night of the day I laid my best friend to rest. I heard a creak of the door and a knock at the window and then a smash. I called for my mum but I couldn't hear my own voice. Someone was calling me louder and louder. I felt hair swoop across my neck and then a smack on my face, hard and cold. My best friend was alive. I should be overjoyed, but no, because it was me that had tried to kill her!

MEGAN FAWCETT (14)
Ullswater Community College, Penrith

THE CAMPOUT

The thick, dark fog made the backyard creepy and scary. My friends and I were camping in the yard of the old house on our street. The night was dark so we went to sleep. All of a sudden, we heard a blood-curdling scream. Alex walked out of the tent to see what the noise was. We screamed and fell into the tent! We all screamed. Slowly the tent's zip moved, it was a young girl with a bloodstained knife. We went to grab a torch but she got into the tent with us...

ELLIOT KITCHEN (13)
Ullswater Community College, Penrith

NOTHING THERE

Something was there, I felt it. It touched me. One side of me was cold and the other warm. I ran, I didn't know what else to do. Suddenly, something tripped me over. I looked, there was nothing there. A cold wind came rushing in. My heart felt like it was going to explode like a bomb. Something was trying to pull me but there was nothing there. All alone. Suddenly, my feet had gone, then my legs, then my chest. My head was the only thing left... then I disappeared!

DAISY BLUNDELL (12)
Ullswater Community College, Penrith

DARKNESS

Darkness crept in like a sinister shadow. It filled the room with an eerie feeling. Something ran in front of me. I stumbled for my torch. Panic ran through my body. I couldn't move, I couldn't breathe. I didn't know what to do. I was alone, I had no one. I tried to run, I tried to scream. It grabbed me. I felt eyes look at me. I felt like they had been watching me for a while. There was nothing I could do. There was nothing I could say. It was too late...

SUMMER LATHAM (14)
Ullswater Community College, Penrith

THE COLD DEMON

As the new owner of this establishment I am going to find out the truth of the cold demon who apparently walks the corridors. As I go up the creaky stairs, I hear it, the beast is right behind me. I can feel their cold breath on my neck and I feel a hand touch my shoulder. I turn to see a mangled body and a kitchen knife right through its heart. Terrified, I run up the stairs to find the body of another victim just lying there. Then I know what my fate will be...

KITTY NICOLSON (13)

Ullswater Community College, Penrith

Watch Your Step!

'Help!' But nobody answered. Then a shriek of laughter pealed. He went to grab his phone but when he tried to ring someone he had no service. He turned the torch on on his phone and saw he was in a dark room. Spiders were crawling up the walls. He climbed a staircase. *Bang!* He ended up on the floor in a pile of blood. He saw a figure by the door. He screamed even louder and then all the spiders on the wall started to run towards him...

Lola Elizabeth Hewitt (11)
Ullswater Community College, Penrith

DEAD HOUSE

One gloomy night, I was walking home. I fell through a portal that looked like a puddle. I was at home. I heard a scream. It was my mum. She was dead. I went through to her room, she had been shot. I heard my baby brother cry. I went through to my room, he was dead. I walked down the stairs. I saw the TV was on. I saw my sister dead, with a knife in her. I saw on the the the wall: 'You're next!' in blood. I ran out the house... 'Argh!'

JACK GRAHAM (12)
Ullswater Community College, Penrith

THE WALKING DEAD

'Mum, Mum, where are we?' There was no reply.
What's going on? I thought to myself. I could hear a
helicopter, I just couldn't justify what it was like. My eyes
were glued shut. I managed to open my eyes, I was in an
army camp with loads of troops everywhere. I got up and
started to walk around. I found my mum, she started to walk
over to the fence. Mum was let out, I started to run towards
her, but it was too late!

LOUIS DAVIDSON (12)
Ullswater Community College, Penrith

THE HAUNTED CHILLER

I was walking down the street alone. I stumbled on a house and knocked, no answer. I checked the door, it was open. I shouted, no answer. I went to the rotten, creaky staircase. All of a sudden, I felt like someone was watching me. I checked every room, no one. Then I went into the bedroom and checked the drawers, nothing. Dressing table, a knife! Bed had blood in it. Under the bed, a dead body. Then I checked the cupboard... 'Argh!'

KIERAN JAMIE DIXON (12)
Ullswater Community College, Penrith

My Worst Nightmare

Black misty fog was slithering through the sky. I was discombobulated; where was I? I came across a black, abandoned house. It was disturbing! The door handle snapped. I kicked the door open with anger. There in front of me was a broken staircase. I didn't know what to do. Noises were hanging in the cold air, things were moving, I knew I was not safe there. A hand touched my shoulder. 'Who's there... ?'

Kyle Strand (14)
Ullswater Community College, Penrith

TRAPPED

The door creaked open, Harry slowly walked in... Out of nowhere, a man jumped out and grabbed Harry and dragged him into a room with cracks and holes in the walls and cobwebs in every corner. The man shoved Harry onto a small wooden chair and pulled a knife from his pocket. Harry screamed and closed his eyes. A while after, Harry opened his eyes and the man was gone. Harry tried to make an escape, but was trapped...

LILY KITCHING (12)
Ullswater Community College, Penrith

THE LOST BOY

The fog was creeping up my legs, the suspense was getting to me and it seemed like a good idea but I kept on hearing noises in the back of my head and then... A girl screamed and I replied, 'Who goes there?' There was no reply. Then out of nowhere there was a church. All the windows were not demolished. But the rest was damaged and a woman was there. As soon as I blinked she was gone and then I was gone.

AARON CAVAGHAN (12)
Ullswater Community College, Penrith

THE DARK LANE

I was walking home down the back lane when I heard footsteps behind me. When I turned around nothing was there. 'Zoe? Is that you?' I carried on walking down through the rustling trees when I heard it again, this time it sounded faster and faster with every step. I was soon running like the wind to get home until a cold hand grabbed my shoulder and pushed me to the cold, hard floor...

LUCY HODGSON (14)
Ullswater Community College, Penrith

HAUNTED EYES

Ike was chasing me into a house, but it wasn't just a house, it was a haunted house. I went in, but it was creepy. I shivered, I was petrified. I went up the stairs, the windows were smashed to smithereens. When I got up there, there were pictures of Shakespeare but they were alive! I ran away from the alive pictures that were following me with their eyes.

BÉLANNA BRAITHWAITE (11)

Ullswater Community College, Penrith

DEATH BY HELL

It was winter and I was playing late at night. The wind was cold. I heard a loud noise. I was scared. I started to panic. I started to run. The noise got louder and louder. I ran faster and faster. The noise got closer and closer. I stopped and looked around. There was no one. I heard a final noise before it grabbed me and pulled me into Hell.

DANIEL CLAUDIO CARCU (13)

Ullswater Community College, Penrith

DANCING TERROR

As I crept through the forest I heard the howling of the wind. At that moment I turned around and all I could see was the fog consuming all the trees. But out of the corner of my eyes I saw the fog break and a shadow of a man appear. 'Who are you?' I screamed. Then he started coming towards me, faster. It was a colossal man...

LUKE COULSTON (11)

Ullswater Community College, Penrith

Cold Scary Night

As the wind blew roughly, I was standing there, freezing. I was lost. I didn't know what to do. My mum said she was on her way. Honestly I had no idea where I was. The weather got colder and colder. My mum couldn't find her way to me either, I lost signal. I felt like something was approaching me. I was right...

Oliwia Waluk (13)

Ullswater Community College, Penrith

THE MYSTERIOUS BUILDING

'Ellis?' my voice echoed desperately down the cobweb-filled hallway. An empty reply. Eerily, a grey mist tangled its way around the portraits either side of me. A sudden chill tingled my bones. What was this place? I looked back as I was leaving and the whole building vanished into thin air.

DANIEL DICKINSON (14)

Ullswater Community College, Penrith

YoungWriters
Est.1991

YOUNG WRITERS
INFORMATION

We hope you have enjoyed reading this book – and
that you will continue to in the coming years.

If you're a young writer who enjoys reading and creative writing, or the
parent of an enthusiastic poet or story writer, do visit our website
www.youngwriters.co.uk. Here you will find free
competitions, workshops and games, as well as
recommended reads, a poetry glossary and our blog.

If you would like to order further copies of this book, or any of our other
titles, then please give us a call or visit **www.youngwriters.co.uk.**

Young Writers
Remus House
Coltsfoot Drive
Peterborough
PE2 9BF
(01733) 890066 / 898110
info@youngwriters.co.uk